# Picker McClikker

by **Allen Johnson, Jr.**
illustrated by **Stephen Hanson**

## PREMIUM PRESS AMERICA
NASHVILLE, TENNESSEE

*To Tillman Franks,*
*who has done so much for country music*

PICKER McCLIKKER
by Allen Johnson, Jr.

Copyright © 1996 by Allen Johnson, Jr

PREMIUM PRESS AMERICA
P.O. Box 159015
Nashville, TN 37215-9015

ISBN 1–887654–14–3

Library of Congress Catalog Card Number 96–68190

PREMIUM PRESS AMERICA books are available at special discounts for premiums, sales promotions, fund–raising, or educational use. For details contact the Publisher at P.O. Box 159015, Nashville, TN 37215–9015; or phone (800) 891–7323.

Created by Allen Johnson, Jr.
Illustrated by Stephen Hanson
Production and design by Our House
The text of this book is set in 13 point Goudy Bold

Printed by Horowitz/Rae Book Manufacturers, Inc.
First Edition, October 1996

# INTRODUCTION

Hey kids!  I'm Marty Stuart, and I want to introduce you to my buddy, Picker McClikker.

I got interested in Picker for several reasons.  He's a fun little guy with a talent, and thanks to a lot of hard work and a warm and loving family who helps him, he becomes a successful musician.  Picker's a little bit like me. I never was fast picking cotton or grapes, but I started playing music when I was nine years old, and like Picker, I went on to see my dream of being a country music artist come true.

Picker and I have another thing in common, a love of hound dogs.  Picker has his lazy, lovable old bloodhound named "Bone," and I have a wonderful bloodhound named Oscar Lee Perkins.

As you know, Picker is make-believe, but one of the characters in the book is real.  The man who gets Picker on The Old Time Hayride radio show is Tillman Franks, an old friend of mine who was really involved in the early days of country music and who knew me when I was just starting as a performer.  It was fun to see Tillman in a book, and it made me realize that Picker would be a good way for kids to find out about country music.

I know you will get as much fun out of Picker as I have.  Remember, each of you has some kind of talent, and if you work hard like Picker, you, too, can do great things.  If Picker McClikker inspires you to know more about country music, you can look in the back of the book and read a piece I have written for you about country music and its heritage.

Your friend,

Marty Stuart

Howdy, kids! My name's Johnny McClikker. I'm fixin' to tell you about my little brother, Picker, but first, you need to know about the McClikker family.

We were all growing up during the 1930's when times were hard. Daddy farmed about a hundred acres of cotton on shares, which meant that he didn't own the land and had to give back part of the crop in rent.

We lived in a little frame house with a tin roof, and we had a big oak shade tree out front that helped to keep the front porch cool in the summer. There was a red dirt farm road that ran near the house with a barbed wire fence alongside that was covered in honeysuckle. In the summer it smelled just wonderful. We lived in the country near Evergreen, Alabama.

There never was much money, but Daddy made enough to buy cornmeal and dried black-eyed peas, and we had a cow and chickens, and Mamma grew sweet corn and greens and such, so there was usually enough to eat.

Daddy raised a hog now and then, so sometimes we had ham or bacon. Sometimes there was a bone for our dog whose *name* was Bone, which was short for bone-lazy. It was a family joke. Mamma'd say, "Johnny, give that bone to Bone," and we always thought it was funny.

There were five of us McClikker kids—three boys and two girls. There was me, Johnny McClikker, Jr., Rufus, Sally, Amy Lou, and Joe, the littlest. I was ten, Rufus seven, Sally six, Amy Lou four, and Joe two-and-a-half. I helped Daddy in the fields after school, and Rufus and Sally did chores, but Amy Lou and Joe were so young they mostly played around the yard.

One evening in early summer we had finished supper and were all sitting on the front porch enjoying the cool and smelling the honeysuckle. Daddy was in the swing with his banjo, puffin' on his pipe and strummin' a chord or two.

Mamma was in the rocker with Amy Lou standing by her knee and the rest of us were playing when Bone slunk up on the porch. He had gotten into a patch of burrs and was stuck up with 'em something awful, from his whiskers to his tail.

We all started to laugh, and Bone sat down looking mighty sad. When we stopped, Joe, who could just walk, toddled over to Bone and sat down, *kerplop*, and said: "Poor Bone. I gonna fix him."

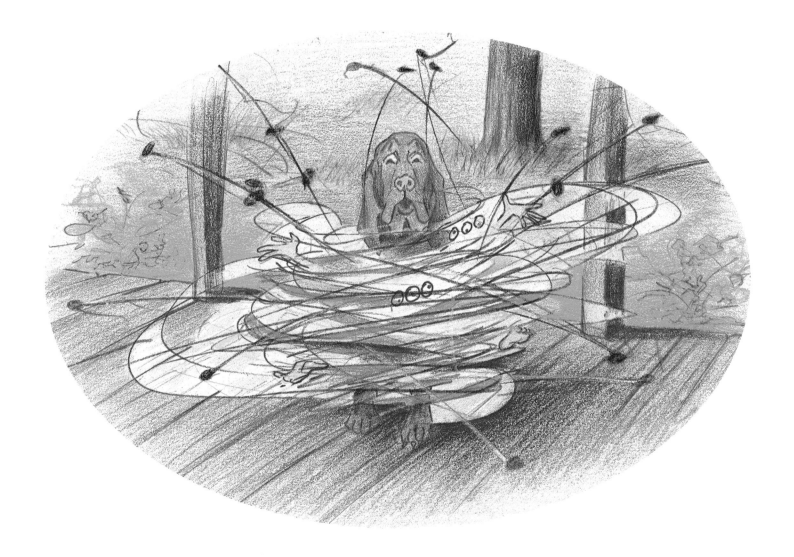

We were all watching when he reached his hands to Bone and then, it's hard to say exactly what happened, but his hands seemed to move like a blur. Then there was some dog hair drifting around in the air and a pile of burrs on the floor. Bone was clean as a whistle, waggin' his tail and practically grinning!  Joe said: "Me fix him."

"What in the world," Daddy said. "Alice, did you see that?"

"I think I did," said Mamma, "but I don't believe it! Did baby Joe just pick about a hundred burrs off Bone in about three seconds?"

"I think he *did*, Alice. Fast! I've never seen the like . . . that boy's a pickin' fool. He's a natural born picker."

"Picker McClikker!" Rufus said. The name stuck, and Joe was "Picker" from then on.

Well, kids, Picker used to help Mamma in the garden picking peas and beans. He was such a peaceful, dreamy little guy that it was hard to believe how fast he was with his hands. It wasn't 'til Picker was almost four years old that we really found out what he could do.

It was during the cotton harvest; Daddy and us older kids had come out of the fields to get some lunch when we noticed the sky getting real black over in the west. It looked like a bad storm was coming. We only had half the crop in, and Daddy was worried. He said we should just grab a bite to eat and get back in the field to try to save the rest of the crop. We knew we'd never do it, though. Picker was tuggin' on Daddy's overalls.

"Picker help!" Daddy looked down.

"What, Son? Oh, thank you, Son. I know how good you can pick, but you're too young to work in the fields."

"No, Daddy, I can help!"

"O.K., son, *everybody* can help! You come, too, Alice. Johnny, run to the barn and get the rest of the bags. Throw 'em in the wagon and hitch up Glory. Bring the wagon out and meet us in the south field!"

By the time I got back to the field with the wagon, the lightning was poppin' and the thunder was whangin' . . . way too close for comfort. Glory was skittish, and I had my hands full keeping her from running off. There was a little dust cloud up ahead movin' down the rows.

When I got closer, I saw it was Picker, going through the cotton like a small tornado. Sally was handing him empty bags. She'd hand him one, and Picker would have it full before she could grab another one.

We all quit pickin' and followed along after Picker, loading the full bags of cotton onto the wagon. It took Picker about fifteen minutes to clean the rest of that field! Our mule, Glory, was all lathered up from runnin' the wagon to the barn and back, and I had a sore rear end from bouncing on the wagon seat. But we got the crop in!

We made it to the porch just as the storm hit, and us kids cheered while Mamma and Daddy danced around with Picker on Daddy's shoulders. The rain blew in, but we were hot and sweaty and it felt *wonderful!*

A few days later, we got a visit from Amos Burdash, the editor of the town newspaper, *The Courant.*

It was Saturday afternoon when Amos stopped by.

"Howdy, Amos," Daddy said, "come on up on the porch and set a spell."

"Can't set, John," Mr. Burdash said. "Too excited. I got to ask you something, John. Your neighbor, Will Crocker, saw Picker in the cotton field last week. Said he never saw anything like it. Do you reckon Picker could pick grapes?"

"Picker can pick *anything*," Daddy said. "Why do you want to know, Amos?"

Mr. Burdash said, "John, I've got an idea. You probably never heard about it, but there's a big grape picking contest in France next month . . . ."

"France!" Daddy hollered, "Amos, you must be . . . ."

"Listen, John. There's a prize, cash money, five thousand dollars! I think this boy of yours could win it." Daddy sat down in the swing lookin' like he'd been hit between the eyes with a two-by-four.

"Lord, Amos, that's a lot of money! You must be foolin' me. I could never get Picker over to France. I can barely keep shoes on these young'uns, much less buy a ticket to France."

"Not one ticket, John, *two*. One for Picker and one for Alice, but the newspaper will pay for the trip. Here is something else. The champion grape picker in France is a 300-pound Gypsy called Big Louis Girard. Look here, I got a picture of him. Think what a story it would be if Big Louis got beat by a four-year-old from Alabama! It could put Evergreen on the map!"

"Lord!" said Daddy, who seemed to be pared down to one word, then Mamma chimed in.

"France, John, just think of it! I've never been farther than Montgomery. Oh, John, can we go?"

I guess it finally sunk in on Daddy 'cause he leaned back in the swing with a twinkle in his eye, and he grinned at Mamma fondly.

"Alice, I'm gonna miss you bad, but there ain't no way on God's green earth I'd let you miss out on going to France." Good thing there was a strong chain on the swing 'cause Mamma jumped in his lap and gave him such a kiss that us kids got embarrassed.

A week later, Mamma and Picker caught the train for New York City, and two days after they got there, they got on a big boat that took them over the Atlantic Ocean to France.

Mamma said it was embarrassing when they got to Bordeaux, France, and met Big Louis. Instead of shaking hands with Picker, Big Louis fell on the ground holding his sides, laughing 'til tears poured down his face, stopping only long enough to point at Picker in amazement . . .

only to start laughing all over again. It made Picker mad, which was hard to do. Picker said to Mamma, "Mr. Big Louis ain't gonna laugh so hard tomorrow," which was the longest sentence anybody had ever heard out of Picker.

Well, the next day, they were out in the vineyard early. Each picker in the contest had his own row of grapes in a big square field. All the rows were the same length. Whoever got to the end first was gonna be the champion. Big Louis had heard that Picker had never picked grapes before and started to laugh all over again.

Big Louis told the judges to take Picker over to another field and let him practice, so he wouldn't be embarrassed in the contest.

Picker stood there with his arms folded over his chest. "No, thank you, Mr. Judge. Picker don't need practice." True! Very true, as it turned out.

The judge fired the gun to start the contest, and Big Louis was just finishing off his fourth vine when another gun went off at the end of the field. Picker had finished. Big Louis looked stunned.

"Mon Dieu!" he said. "C'est impossible!"(Which means something like, "Lord have mercy! That's impossible!")

It was quite a shock for Big Louis, but he turned out to have a heart as big as the rest of him 'cause when Picker got the prize, Big Louis said it was an honor to be beaten by "Monsieur Piquer," the greatest "piquer" that the world would ever know. ("Piquer" was as close as the French could come to "Picker." It sounded something like "Pee-cur!")

Picker loved France, but he said he didn't like being called no Pee-cur! Anyway, there was a victory parade and Big Louis carried Picker all around Bordeaux on his shoulder while folks cheered and threw flowers. Two weeks later the world's champion grape picker came home to Evergreen, Alabama.

It did put Evergreen on the map, too. All the big newspapers picked up the story of the
champion grape picker. Picker was famous, but he didn't seem to care. He just went right back to
being a normal little boy, only more dreamy and peaceful than most. Daddy wanted to put the prize
money in the bank for Picker to have for college, but Picker said he wanted us to own our piece of

land and little house, so Daddy used the money for that, but he put the house and land in Picker's name. There was enough left over for Daddy to buy the tractor, so he could farm a little easier and our hard working mule, Glory, could retire. Then Picker went downtown with Mamma and bought us all something.

Mamma got some pretty new dresses and we all got new clothes and shoes, but we each got something special, too. Amy Lou got a beautiful doll; Sally, who was a tomboy, got a baseball glove and ball; and me and Rufus got Red Ryder BB guns. Boy, that was exciting! Then Daddy asked Picker what *he* wanted.

"Picker want a pretty banjo like Daddy plays," he said.

"Why shore!" said Daddy. "No reason why a champion picker can't pick a banjo."

Daddy started right in giving Picker banjo lessons and even made a little wooden stand to hold the banjo, 'cause Picker just wasn't big enough to hold it.

Well, sir, as Picker grew up, it wasn't long before he had learned to play everything that Daddy knew.

"Alice," Daddy said to Mamma, "I can't teach this child no more. I got to get him some sure enough lessons. What do you think about Slim Tuttle? He's the best player around these parts, and he's a real nice man. I just know he'd like to teach Picker the banjo."

"That's a good idea, John," Mamma said, "but Slim lives in Frisco City. That's too far to walk. Maybe Picker could ride over there with Bill Pratt on the newspaper truck. Bill goes to Frisco City every Thursday."

So that's how Picker got lessons from Slim Tuttle for the next four years.

Well, kids, by the time Picker was eight years old, he had gotten so good that Slim decided to put him in a banjo contest. Some folks laughed when Picker set up the banjo on the little stand Daddy had made but Picker just stepped right up and played "Mississippi Sawyer" pretty as you please. Slim wasn't surprised that Picker won. In fact, while Picker was playing, Slim was over talking to Daddy about getting Picker a chance to play on the radio. Slim said he was going to call his old friend, Tillman Franks, who played bass fiddle on *The Old Time Hayride* radio show that was broadcast on KWKH out of Shreveport, Louisiana.

About a week after Picker turned nine, Slim had come for supper. After we ate, Slim and Picker and Daddy played us some music on the front porch. It was mighty pretty. Then Slim gave us some good news.

"Alice," Slim said, "you and John remember I called Tillman Franks about Picker playing on the *Hayride?* Well, Tillman called me back today, said if I can get Picker to Shreveport on Saturday they could try him out and if they like his playing, they can put him on the show that same night."

"Heck, Slim, that's wonderful," Daddy said. "Picker can miss one day of school. How about it son, you want to try it?"

"Yes, sir!" said Picker. "Can Bone come along for company?"
"Don't see why not," said Slim. "We'll put him in the rumble seat."
Well, kids, the rest is history.

When Picker appeared on *The Old Time Hayride*, Tillman Franks let Bone go on stage, too. Trouble was, Bone went to sleep! Picker stepped up to the microphone and played "Arkansas Traveler." When the audience heard Picker playing like a house afire and saw Bone asleep at his feet, they got tickled.

They started laughing and clapping and stomping so much it woke up Bone, who pushed

himself up on his front paws and started to howl! Then the audience really cut loose. Picker and Bone were quite a hit.

You kids know how famous Picker got. Made a lot of money, too, making records and playing on the radio. None of that changed him, though. Fact is, Picker used quite a bit of the money he made to help us other kids get set up in life.

    'Course Picker's growed up now. Fact is, he married Caroline Bridewell from over in Burnt Corn, Alabama. Caroline's a little bitty gal but strong-minded and got a good head for business. Good thing too 'cause Picker's as dreamy as ever and won't pay much attention to money.

    Caroline and Picker built a house on the farm near Mamma and Daddy who're mighty glad to have the company. Last fall Caroline had a baby, and they named him Joe junior after Picker who's real name was Joe, and kids, just yesterday Picker called me on the phone and told me something real

interesting. Said that Caroline had asked Mamma and Daddy over for supper. Picker said that after supper Caroline was getting a pie out of the oven when Mamma decided to hand baby Joe a pacifier. She had it in her hand reaching for baby Joe, when it just disappeared. She looked down and there it was in the baby's mouth, but she never saw it get there. Well, I know what *that* means. We're all hoping that baby Joe grows up taking a shine to the guitar. Banjo and guitar is a mighty pretty sound.

# THE HERITAGE OF COUNTRY MUSIC
## by Marty Stuart

Maybe you dream of becoming a professional athlete, a doctor, lawyer, nurse, or scientist. When I was young, I dreamed of becoming a country music singer. My hero was Johnny Cash because he sang songs about interesting people and places around the world. After I saw him in person at a concert, I knew that what he was doing was what I wanted to do with my life. Somewhere along the way, my dream came true; now I get to travel all over the world to play and sing country music. I love it.

The earliest country music came to America with our ancestors, who immigrated from England, Scotland, Ireland, and Africa. It was played on banjos, fiddles, mandolins, string basses, dulcimers, and autoharps. As America grew, songwriters wrote songs about its stories of triumph, tragedy, love, and pure fun. These songs were enjoyed by people from all walks of life. Country music has been called "the music of the people" because of the stories in the songs. The messages are simple and easy to understand.

The first recordings of this music were made in the 1920's. Record producers in search of "something different" would take their recording machines out into the rural areas of the South and visit musicians and singers in their homes or on their porches. Sometimes producers would advertise and invite the local performers to come to a hotel and audition for a chance to make a phonograph record. That's how the country music recording and publishing industries, as well as the nation's first generation of country music stars, were born.

Two of the most popular acts from this period of time were the Carter Family from Virginia and Jimmie Rodgers from Meridian, Mississippi. Jimmie Rodgers, often called "The Singing Brakeman," was the first country superstar. He influenced generations of future singers and is commonly known as "The Father of Country Music."

Every region of the country had its characters and stylists. One of the strongest music styles to emerge from the West was called "western swing," which was made popular by a Texan named Bob Wills. It combined fiddle music and country lyrics with dance orchestra instruments. The West also produced cowboy stars who pioneered a type of music referred to as "Country-Western." Movie stars like Roy Rogers and Gene Autry, referred to as "The Singing Cowboys," helped make country music popular in the 1950's. Millions of people paid their nickels and dimes to watch these cowboys—in between singing songs—fight bad guys, rescue pretty girls, and restore law and order.

The true heart and soul of country music came from the foothills of the Appalachian Mountains.

Bill Monroe created one of the most exciting, strong band styles of music. He called it "Bluegrass," in honor of his home state of Kentucky. Bluegrass music is fast and powerful. It combines sounds of church, heavenly singing, fiddle tunes, and lonesome ballads with the Blues—another style of music. One of Bill Monroe's most famous songs is "Blue Moon of Kentucky." In 1955, years after he had first recorded it, a rock and roll singer named Elvis Presley also recorded it, and it launched his career.

A number of famous country musicians got their start with Bill Monroe's band, the Bluegrass Boys. Two of the biggest stars were Lester Flatt and Earl Scruggs. I'm glad for their success because many years later, when I was 13 years old, Lester Flatt gave me my first job in Nashville. As a young person learning his trade, I was fortunate to have had full access to the knowledge and wisdom of some of these architects of country music. Being around those pioneers was the equivalent of a young artist working in the presence of Picasso or Michelangelo.

Much of country music's experience comes from its roots of gospel music and its association with the church. The influence of gospel music is heard in the music of Bill Monroe, Hank Williams, Patsy Cline, Wynonna Judd, Alison Krauss, and Travis Tritt.

One of the dearest churches ever associated with country music is the Ryman Auditorium in Nashville. It is a meeting house that was built by a riverboat captain named Thomas Ryman. Through the years, it has served both as a church and theater. From 1943-1974, it was the home of the *Grand Ole Opry*, country music's most famous radio show. The *Opry* got its name when, after an evening's broadcast of opera and classical music, a man named George D. Hay (or "The Solemn Old Judge," as he was called) announced that instead of grand opera, listeners would be hearing "Grand Ole Opry." Imagine what thousands of radio listeners must have thought when they heard people having fun, telling jokes, and making mountain music just like they always had back home. Radio station WSM, called "The Air Castle of the South," has broadcast the *Opry* since the show was founded in 1925. It beams a 50,000-watt clear channel signal throughout the southland and on into the heart of America.

The Ryman Auditorium went on to be known as "The Mother Church of Country Music." The *Opry* became the place where all of the different styles of country music that had been developing could come together in common purpose. The public developed a loving affection for the comedy, sacred songs, cowboy songs, fiddle songs, banjo songs, sad songs, and happy songs performed by colorful characters at the *Opry*. It has become the most prestigious fraternity in country music.

Many other shows were patterned after the *Opry*, but none came as close in popularity as the *Louisiana Hayride*, which was broadcast every weekend on radio station KWKH in Shreveport, Louisiana. The Hayride was called "The Cradle of the Stars" because as soon as performers became popular, they left to join the *Grand Ole Opry*. Stars like Hank Williams, Kitty Wells, and Jim Reeves all got their start with the *Louisiana Hayride*. The show was so popular that the *Hayride's* manager, Tillman Franks, once called Shreveport "the country soul of the whole wide world."

After all these years and all of the stars who have come and gone, the two most beloved performers were Roy Acuff and Minnie Pearl. We all owe a debt of gratitude to Mr. Acuff for giving country music credibility. He was one of the first country stars to be known worldwide, carrying his music to places and people that had never heard of country music. A friend to a number of American presidents, his thoughts and values of home, family, and religious faith reflected the conscience of country music throughout his entire life.

Ask any of the ladies in country music—Reba McEntire, Dolly Parton, or Faith Hill—who helped pave the way for women and they will no doubt tell you how much they admire Sarah Ophelia Cannon, a lady of dignity and social graces from Grinders Switch, Tennessee. You might know her as "Cousin Minnie Pearl." When it was *Opry* time, she put on old shoes, a checkerboard dress, and a straw hat with a $1.50 price tag hanging on it. She told funny stories about true life friends and relatives, and we always laughed. She made the world brighter, which is what country music is meant to do.

Long before satellites beamed videos 24 hours a day, country performers took their music to the people at schoolhouses, theatres, county fairs, and city auditoriums. In the early days, stars traveled from show to show in cars packed with band members, instruments, and costumes. Today, we travel in customized tour buses and jets, and some artists perform as many as 300 concerts a year. Concerts now need an entire team of people to set up. It usually takes a full day to just prepare the sound system and lighting. Millions of people of all ages attend country concerts each year.

One of the most endearing charms of country music is the family–like atmosphere that has passed from generation to generation. Many country stars can be heard singing and playing on each other's albums and concerts simply for the love and enjoyment of it. As a rule, country stars are friendly people; many of them can be seen signing autographs and mingling with their fans after a concert. True country fans have always been dedicated and loyal to their favorite stars. It is the fans that have always given our music its heartbeat.

Country music is timeless. It belongs to everybody. Songs are magic carpets that take you across the universe. In country music, dreams can come true. I know, and you should know. There's always room for one more dreamer.

# How To Order This Book

If your local bookstore or souvenir shop is out of *Picker McClikker,* and you'd like extra copies for your favorite country music fans, you can order direct by sending a check or money order made payable to PREMIUM PRESS AMERICA in the amount of $8.95 ($6.95 plus $2.00 shipping). Additional copies (at $6.95 each to the same address) are shipped FREE.

SEND TO: Picker McClikker
PREMIUM PRESS AMERICA
P.O. Box 159015
Nashville, TN 37215-9015
(615)256-8484

SPECIAL NOTE: Originally released in two separate hardback editions *Picker McClikker* and *Picker McClikker: The Rest of the Story* are still available in very limited quantity.

The first edition, autographed, hardback books are available at a special discount rate of $11.95 plus $2.00 for shipping.

These hardback editions originally retailed for $16.95 and feature more pages and illustrations. To order send a check made payable to PREMIUM PRESS AMERICA in the amount of $13.95 per book or $24.95 for both books.

LIBRARIANS: There is an additional ten (10%) percent discount for school and public libraries.

Allow 2-4 weeks for delivery.